The Emperor's New Clothes

The Emperor's New Clothes

Retold by Louise John
Illustrated by Serena Curmi

Evans

First published 2009 by
Evans Brothers Limited
2A Portman Mansions
Chiltern St
London W1U 6NR

British Library Cataloguing in Publication Data

John, Louise.
    The emperor's new clothes. - (Skylarks)
    1. Children's stories.
    I. Title II. Series
    823.9'2-dc22

ISBN-13: HB 978 0 237 53908 5
ISBN-13: PB 978 0 237 53895 8

Printed in China by New Era Printing Co. Ltd

Series Editor: Louise John
Design: Robert Walster
Production: Jenny Mulvanny

Contents

Chapter One

There once lived an emperor who was kind and just. He ruled wisely and his people loved him. But the emperor was also proud and vain and liked nothing more than looking at himself in the mirror. He spent all of his money on new clothes – robes in every colour and fabric that you could imagine: bright silks and embroidered satins, all trimmed with fancy frills and feathers.

The emperor's favourite pastime was to ride around in his carriage, showing off his beautiful clothes to anyone who would look. He had different robes for every single hour of every single day.

Time passed merrily and visitors to the emperor's town came and went. Everyone knew about the emperor's fancy wardrobe and people came from far and wide just to admire him.

One fine day, two strangers arrived at the palace. They told the courtiers that they were weavers and asked for permission to see the emperor.

9

"We have travelled the world and learned new skills. We can weave cloth of the most beautiful colours and patterns," they told the emperor.

"It is magical cloth," said one weaver.

"Magical cloth?" breathed the emperor in excitement.

"Cloth that can only be seen by those worthy of their position," said the other.

"I must have this cloth!" gasped the emperor. "I must have it at once!"

So the emperor gave the weavers bags of gold coins as payment. They set up their looms in the palace and demanded the best silk and threads, and the finest spun gold. And they set to work.

But the two scoundrels put nothing on their looms. Instead, they stuffed the silk and thread into their pockets and the looms stood empty. Then, the two crooks sat down and, with looks of great concentration on their faces, they pretended to weave.

Chapter Two

Day after day the weavers worked, sitting at the empty looms pretending to weave. Night after night, they took home their bags of gold coins and emptied their pockets of the gold thread and silk they had stolen.

The emperor's courtiers watched all

this in amazement. But no one dared to say a word.

Soon enough, the emperor could contain his excitement no longer. He was, however, a little worried. What if he, of all people, could not see the cloth? What if he, the emperor, was proved to be not worthy of his position?

14

Nonsense, he thought to himself. Whoever heard of such a thing!

But, just to be on the safe side, the emperor made a plan.

"I will send my best minister to see the cloth," he decided. "He is honest, sensible and hard-working. He does an excellent job and is definitely worthy of his position. I can trust him to tell me the truth."

So, the trusted minister went along to check on the cloth. He watched in astonishment as the two crooks sat at their empty looms, pretending to work away.

The minister could not believe his eyes.

"Where on earth is the cloth?" he muttered to himself. "I see nothing.

I see nothing at all!"

"Come closer," said the first of the weavers. "Come and admire our work!"

He pointed at the empty loom and encouraged the minister to examine the colours, the pattern and the beautiful quality of the cloth.

The minister stared. First at the weaver, and then at the empty loom.

He stared as hard as he dared, but still he could not see the beautiful cloth that the weaver talked about. Because there was nothing there for him to see!

The minister hung his head in shame. I am a fool, a fraud. I am not worthy of my position as the emperor's minister, he thought to himself.

"So what do you think?" asked the second weaver. "Do you think our cloth will please the emperor?"

"Indeed it will," smiled the minister, peering at the loom again. "It is the most beautiful cloth I have ever seen."

And he listened again carefully as the weavers explained the detail of the pattern and named all the colours. The emperor would want to know every last detail.

"No one must ever know. It would never do to tell the emperor that I could not see the cloth," he mumbled to himself. "It will be my secret."

"Excellent, excellent!" he said aloud. "The cloth is coming along very well indeed. I will hurry to tell the emperor immediately."

Chapter Three

The emperor was overjoyed to hear about the progress his cloth was making, not to mention very relieved indeed that his minister could actually see the magical cloth. There was nothing to worry about, after all.

He listened with delight as the

minister talked about the beautiful colours and patterns.

"I can't wait to see this magical cloth!" the emperor exclaimed. "I shall use it to make the finest robes I have ever owned!"

Soon enough the two rogues were demanding even more money to buy their supplies of silk and golden thread. They needed it, they said, to finish the cloth but, of course, not a single thread appeared on the looms and all the money disappeared into their own pockets. Every day, though, the weavers continued to move their hands at the empty looms, pulling and twisting the imaginary thread this way and that.

After some time, the emperor's curiosity got the better of him, and he decided to send another of his ministers to see how the weaving was going.

"You must ask them how much longer it will take," instructed the emperor. "I am getting impatient to have my cloth!"

But the same thing happened again.

No matter how hard the minister looked, he could see no sign at all of the magical cloth.

"What do you think?" asked the pair of swindlers. "Isn't it lovely? It is the finest cloth you will ever see, that's for sure."

Either my eyes are tricking me, thought the man to himself, or I am no good at my job and not worthy to serve the emperor.

He began to panic. "No one must know I cannot see this cloth. I have

worked for the emperor for many years, and would be ashamed if he knew I am not worthy of my position."

So, turning to the weavers again, he began the same pretence as the minister before him.

"Indeed it is beautiful," he gushed, stretching out his hand into thin air to touch the imaginary cloth and making admiring noises. "Exquisite colours and such a handsome design!"

He went directly to the emperor and reported, "I could not take my eyes off the cloth, such was its beauty. It held me mesmerised!"

"Excellent news!" smiled the emperor and clapped his hands together in excitement. "I cannot believe my good fortune."

Chapter Four

Word spread like wildfire and soon the
cloth was the talk of the whole town.
The emperor decided that the time had
come to look at the cloth for himself.
He wanted to admire it whilst it was still
on the loom.

So, one fine morning, he gathered a

small group of his men together, including the two ministers who had been sent to see the cloth before, and went to the weaving room.

As before, the two scoundrels sat at their empty looms pretending to weave away busily.

27

The emperor could not believe his eyes. He opened his mouth to protest, and then quickly shut it again, as he realised that his two ministers could see the cloth.

"Look at the fine colours," said the first.

"Magnificent!" said the other.

The other men joined in, all believing that the others could see the fabric, and not wanting to be the first to admit that there was nothing there.

"I have never seen quality like it," said another, reaching out a hand to stroke the air.

29

What is this tomfoolery? thought the emperor. I can't see anything at all. This is terrible! Am I a fool? Am I unfit to be emperor?

After a long silence, he joined in with his ministers.

"Yes, this cloth has my highest approval," he smiled to the weavers. "Carry on, men. Do not let us keep you from such important work."

On the way back to his chambers, the emperor was deep in thought. No one must guess that he saw nothing on the looms at all. It would be the undoing of him.

After a sleepless night, he had the idea to give the weavers a medal to reward them for their hard work and great talent. He would give them each the title of 'Master Weaver'. Surely no one would doubt that he could see the cloth after such a generous gesture.

Chapter Five

Excitement about the cloth grew and grew and the emperor's courtiers and ministers persuaded the emperor to wear an outfit made from the new cloth in a procession that was to take place the following week.

Before the procession, the two

swindlers sat up all night and burned
more than sixteen candles, to show how
hard they were working to finish the
emperor's new clothes on time. In the
morning, rubbing their sleep-filled eyes,
they held up the garments for everyone
to admire.

"The clothes are ready! This is the coat, these are the trousers and this is the cloak. All as light as a feather, so that the emperor will not even know he is wearing them. This is what makes them such fine quality!"

34

The emperor undressed in front of a long mirror and the rogues pretended to put the new clothes on him. They draped the fabric around him, and murmured approval as they fastened imaginary buttons and smoothed imaginary creases.

"How well Your Majesty's new clothes look," said the first weaver.

"What a perfect fit," said the other.

And all around him, as he twisted and turned in front of the mirror, admiring cries filled the room about how splendid the emperor looked in his fine new clothes.

No matter how hard he looked, the emperor could still not see the clothes.

No matter how hard they looked, the courtiers could still not see the clothes.

But no one was going to be the first to admit it, and so it was that the emperor stood there naked before the weavers, wearing nothing more than the suit he had been born in!

Chapter Six

The minister of processions stepped forward. "Your Imperial Highness, the canopy awaits outside," he said.

"Well," said the emperor, who was secretly a little reluctant. "I am ready. I agree that these clothes are an excellent fit and the finest I have ever owned.

Let the procession begin…"

He glanced behind him to take one long last look in the mirror, as two of his courtiers bent down and lifted up the imaginary train on his cloak. They dared not admit there was nothing to hold.

So, off went the emperor in procession

under his splendid canopy. The people in the streets were taken aback at first, but quickly pulled themselves together and began to call out to the emperor.

"See how magnificent he looks!"

"Look at his long train!"

"Such elegance and style!"

For, just like the ministers, and indeed

the emperor himself, no one dared to speak out. To admit to the truth would have shown them to be fools.

No costume that the emperor had ever worn before had been so well received. The crowds clapped and cheered and the emperor walked proudly on, though he did feel a little chilly!

Suddenly, in a quiet moment, a little boy's voice was heard.

"Daddy, look, the emperor has nothing on!" he said loudly.

The child's father was embarrassed and, turning to his neighbours, said, "Did you ever hear such nonsense? Goodness me, what silly things children say…"

But, slowly but surely, a whisper moved through the crowd, growing louder and louder.

"That child says the emperor hasn't got anything on!"

And soon enough the whole town was crying out, "But he hasn't got anything on!"

The emperor stopped and shivered as a cool breeze snaked past his naked body, and he suspected for the first time that they might be right.

"Oh dear," he thought to himself. "What a to-do! But a procession is a procession and it will not do to stop. The show must go on!"

So, he lifted his head proudly, and carried on gaily through the streets. In amazement, his courtiers once again lifted his imaginary train and on went the procession!

43

If you enjoyed this story, why not read another *Skylarks* book?

Josie's Garden
by David Orme and Martin Remphry

Josie lives in a high-rise flat in town with her mum and brother. More than anything else in the world, Josie wants a garden. When Josie and her friend, Meena, discover an abandoned and over-grown garden near their school, Josie is delighted and decides to make the garden her own. But sometimes, things are not quite as simple as they first seem…

Merbaby

by Penny Kendal and Claudia Venturini

One day at the beach, Anna, Ellie and Joe find a funny-looking fish in a rock pool. To their surprise, they find that the fish is a baby mermaid! They take the merbaby home in a bucket and keep it a secret from Mum. But, four-year-old Joe isn't very good at keeping secrets, and soon the merbaby is in danger. Will Anna and Ellie be able to save her?

Noah's Shark
by Alan Durant and Holly Surplice

Noah was fed up with the people in his world making a right mess of everything. He built a big boat to escape in, and invited his animal friends along – couples only! The animals queued up by the boat, two by two. All except for Mrs Shark, who came alone. It seemed she had accidentally eaten her husband! Would Noah be able to trust her on his boat?

Carving the Sea Path
by Kathryn White and Evelyne Duverne

When Samuel first moves to the Arctic, he is rude and unfriendly. But Irniq gives him a chance, and the boys become friends. Then, as the summer comes to an end, the boys quarrel and drift apart. One day, Irniq finds a trapped whale under the ice, and doesn't know what to do. Luckily, Samuel appears and knows exactly who can help. Will the boys save the whale in time?

Skylarks titles include:

Awkward Annie
by Julia Williams and Tim Archbold
HB 9780237533847 / PB 9780237534028

Sleeping Beauty
by Louise John and Natascia Ugliano
HB 9780237533861 / PB 9780237534042

Detective Derek
by Karen Wallace and Beccy Blake
HB 9780237533885 / PB 9780237534066

Hurricane Season
by David Orme and Doreen Lang
HB 9780237533892 / PB 9780237534073

Spiggy Red
by Penny Dolan and Cinzia Battistel
HB 9780237533854 / PB 9780237534035

London's Burning
by Pauline Francis and Alessandro Baldanzi
HB 9780237533878 / PB 9780237534059

The Black Knight
by Mick Gowar and Graham Howells
HB 9780237535803 / PB 9780237535926

Ghost Mouse
by Karen Wallace and Beccy Blake
HB 9780237535827 / PB 9780237535940

Yasmin's Parcels
by Jill Atkins and Lauren Tobia
HB 9780237535858 / PB 9780237535971

Muffin
by Anne Rooney and Sean Julian
HB 9780237535810 / PB 9780237535933

Tallulah and the Tea Leaves
by Louise John and Vian Oelofsen
HB 9780237535841 / PB 9780237535964

The Big Purple Wonderbook
by Enid Richemont and Helen Jackson
HB 9780237535834 / PB 9780237535957

Noah's Shark
by Alan Durant and Holly Surplice
HB 9780237539047 / PB 9780237538910

The Emperor's New Clothes
by Louise John and Serena Curmi
HB 9780237539085 / PB 9780237538958

Carving the Sea Path
by Kathryn White and Evelyn Duverne
HB 9780237539030 / PB 9780237538903

Merbaby
by Penny Kendal and Claudia Venturini
HB 9780237539078 / PB 9780237538941

The Lion and the Gypsy
by Jillian Powell and Heather Deen
HB 9780237539054 / PB 9780237538927

Josie's Garden
by David Orme and Martin Remphry
HB 9780237539061 / PB 9780237538934